CHARLOTTE AGELL

I Swam with a Seal

GULLIVER BOOKS

HARCOURT BRACE & COMPANY

San Diego   New York   London

Requests for permission to make copies of any part of the work
should be mailed to: Permissions Department,
Harcourt Brace & Company, 6277 Sea Harbor Drive,
Orlando, Florida 32887-6777.

Gulliver Books is a registered trademark of Harcourt Brace & Company.

Library of Congress Cataloging-in-Publication Data
Agell, Charlotte.
I swam with a seal/Charlotte Agell. — 1st ed.
p.   cm.
"Gulliver books."
Summary: A child imitates various animals and each one notices
that she is different from them in some way.
ISBN 0-15-200176-X
[1. Animals—Fiction. 2. Stories in rhyme.] I. Title.
PZ8.3.A2595Iaac   1995
[E]—dc20   94-5652

Printed in Singapore

First edition
A B C D E

To Liz Van Doren and
Claire Bottler McKean — Hurrah!

I swam with a seal
in the calm blue sea.
The seal took a good, long
look at me.

Where are your shiny flippers, you funny seal?

I hopped with a hare
in the tall, tall grass.
The hare glanced at me
as if to ask . . .

Where are your floppy ears, you funny hare?

I flew with a falcon
with my feet on the ground.
The falcon sailed by
with hardly a sound.

Where are your broad wings, you funny falcon?

I slithered with a snake
near the old stone wall.
The snake didn't look
at me at all.

Where is your flickering tongue, you funny snake?

I pranced with a pony
in the meadow by the hill.
The pony whinnied
and then was still.

Where is your wild mane, you funny pony?

I bothered a beaver
who was building a dam.
She slapped the water,
and away she swam.

Where is your strong tail, you funny beaver?

I trailed a turtle
by the potting shed.
He spied me,
and in went his head.

Where is your hard shell, you funny turtle?

I giggled with a gull
on the fishing dock.
He was louder,
but we both could squawk.

Where is your gaping beak, you funny gull?

I peeked at a porcupine
in a tall pine tree.
I was hiding,
but he could see.

Where are your sharp quills, you funny porcupine?

I danced with a dog
in the busy park.
She licked my face
and taught me to bark.

Where is your furry coat, you funny dog?

I happened on a heron
fishing in the stream.
She stalked by me,
quiet as a dream.

Where are your long, skinny legs, you funny heron?

I meandered with a moose
in the evening fog.
He hardly looked up
from his meal in the bog.

Where are your proud antlers, you funny moose?

I cuddled with a cat
as the moon shone in.
She purred and purred
and kissed me on the chin.

Where are your tickling whiskers, you funny cat?

We snuggled with our grandpa
in our beds by the light.
He read us a story,
then said, "Good night."

Sleep well and sweet dreams, you funny, funny honeys!

The paintings in this book were done in Winsor & Newton watercolors,
Berol Prismacolor Stix, and India Ink on Arches hot-press watercolor paper.
The display type was set in Bodega Serif Medium by
Harcourt Brace & Company Photocomposition Center, San Diego, California.
The text type was set in Stempel Garamond by Thompson Type, San Diego, California.
Color separations by Bright Arts, Ltd., Singapore
Printed and bound by Tien Wah Press, Singapore
This book was printed with soya-based inks on Leykam recycled paper,
which contains more than 20 percent postconsumer waste and has a
total recycled content of at least 50 percent.
Production supervision by Warren Wallerstein and Ginger Boyer
Designed by Lori J. McThomas